I0567569

# THE CHILDREN OF THE GODS.

## THE HURRICANE'S  BROTHERS

### A CHILDREN'S  STORY

### BY SEMISI  PULE

Copyright © Rainbow Enterprises 2012

Publisher: Rainbow Enterprises 2012

ISBN: 978-1-927308-31-8

All rights reserved. No part of this publication maybe
reproduced or transmitted in any form or by any means,
electronic or mechanical, including photocopy, recording or
any information storage or retrieval system, without
permission in writing from the publisher and copyright holder.
Rainbow Enterprises is the trade/publisher name of Semisi
Pule a.k.a. Semisi Pule Pone.

Distributed by Rainbow Enterprises.

Email: rainbowenterprises7@gmail.com
semisipone@yahoo.com

# CONTENTS.

CHAPTERS

# CHAPTER 1.  THE GIANT FISH

'Etu, Ma, Tupu'a and Langi woke up early one morning to find Latou cooking a large fish on the 'umu fire.

"What is that fish father?", Langi asked.

"This fish is called a Lupo", Latou answered.

"I caught it in my net last night. It does not come this way normally".

"It smells delicious", Langi said.

"Yes it is", answered Latou.

'Etu, Ma and Tupu'a were standing beside the 'umu staring at the fish. They have been resting for about a week after returning from Manono. The Tu'i Tonga Empire has been saved by the Gods. Lafaipana is still stuck to the moon while his army has been brought under control and included in the Tu'i Tonga's overseas "Empire Guards".

"According to legend, the Lupo belonged to the God Maui, then Lupo's brother Afaa brought it to Tongatapu from the land of the Gods. Its descendants are still here today".

"Where is the land of the Gods father?", Langi continued.

"I heard that it is even further than Pulotu. You have to sail for 2 weeks and then you see a longwhite cloud. The land is hidden underneath it. Few people have gone there and returned", Latou answered.

"Why is that?", 'Etu asked

"I heard there are many monsters, whirlpools and other dangers that can destroy your canoe and yourself on the way", Latou answered. "The only way to get there safely is to ask Lupo and Afaa's brother, the Seer to help you. He is the only one that can see everything ahead of you and tell you what to do. That is how Afaa and Lupo got here. The Seer helped them".

"We would love to go there. I would like to meet Maui and the other Gods", Langi said enthusiastically.

"It is a very dangerous journey", Latou warned.

Langi persisted over the coming weeks. 'Etu, Ma, Tupu'a and Mafanga also joined in. They all support Langi's idea. They should go to the land of the Gods for a visit. Latou was firm. He did not like the idea at all.

Then one day 'Etu, Ma and Tupu'a were helping Latou with the nets, they got a bright idea.

"Why don't we go and ask the Seer?", they said. "Maybe he can tell us how to get there. Do you know where to find him?".

"I heard that he may be at the festival of the Giant Fish soon in the Sacred Island", Latou was still feeling scared.

"It is only about a week's travel by canoe father. Why don't we go and talk to him?", 'Etu suggested.

"Let me discuss it with Mafanga tonight, we all have to go", Latou said.

"Alright", the boys agreed, looking happy. They can sense the huge adventure ahead.

The next day they prepared the morning 'umu. 'Etu, collected some firewood. Ma and Tupu'a went to the plantation and brought some yam, taro, coconuts and taro leaves. Latou slaughtered a piglet for roasting.

Mafanga and Langi prepared the lu, after Ma grated and squeezed some coconuts. 'Etu got some banana leaves and toughened them by heating them over the fire to prevent any tearing. It would be used to hold the lu together using the banana leaf ribs.

When the stones were white hot they leveled them, removed any remaining bits of burning wood and put in the food then covered it with banana and giant taro leaves then soil mixed with sand.

Latou started another fire to roast the piglet. It was their favourite meat. They got a long pole and stuck it through the piglet for roasting. A stick with a fork at one end was stuck in the ground by the fire to hold the other end of the pole. 'Etu, Ma and Tupu'a will take turns turning the pole, and the piglet over and over for it to cook evenly.

"We have decided that we should leave this afternoon. That is why we are cooking the piglet. We can take part of it and the leftover taro and yam with us then cook more food after tomorrow", Latou said.

The kids were excited and all started talking at once. "I have to warn you. I do not know what is going to happen. If we find the Seer, we may be able to go", Latou added. "If we can't find him, it might be too dangerous to attempt it".

"We are all willing to try father", 'Etu said.

"Alright. But first let's eat. The Lupo is delicious", Latou said.

After having their mid-morning meal. Latou and the 3 boys started preparations for their journey to Sacred Island. They loaded food, the piglet, water, blankets and some fishing gear onto the biggest and fastest canoe. Mafanga and Langi prepared some sleeping mats and extra tapa if they need to make any clothes or blankets during the journey.

"Looks like everything is ready. We can sail this afternoon", Latou said.

"Yes, we are all ready", Mafanga replied.

"What about you boys?. Have you got anything else to load?", Latou asked 'Etu, Ma and Tupu'a.

"No father, everything has been loaded", 'Etu answered. He was always the one to check and answer Latou as he was the eldest.

"Let's go, then", Latou said.

They dragged the canoe into the water. It was rather large so they had logs at the bottom to make it easy to move. Once in the water, they put the log rollers neatly back under the hibiscus tree beside the beach, and got on the canoe. The boys helped Latou put up the sail and they can feel the canoe picking up speed as Latou steered it out of the lagoon.

A steady breeze was blowing. Mafanga and Langi went down to the sleeping quarters and rested. The boys took turns in helping Latou steer the canoe. It will be a journey of several days.

That night they all slept in the sleeping quarters under the deck. 'Etu stayed up to steer the canoe. He will call Ma to take over when he is tired.

Normally only large Kalias has 2 decks but Latou made one for his canoe to fit in the whole family in 2 compartments.

Next morning was a beautiful clear day. A steady breeze was blowing in a cloudless sky. They all came up on board and admired the rising sun, when suddenly they felt a jolt and the canoe was lifted slightly to almost above sealevel. 'Etu looked over the side and saw a huge shadow underneath the canoe.

"It's the Giant Fish!", he shouted. "It's got the canoe on its back!".

They all looked under the canoe between the hulls and could see the dorsal fins. It was about 3 times longer than the canoe! It was picking up speed. The fish with the canoe on its back was travelling at about 10 times their normal speed.

"I think it's taking us to the Seer", Latou said. "According to legend, the Giant fish is the Seer's brother. Let's just enjoy the ride. Mafanga why don't you and Langi prepare our morning meal?".

After they ate the rest of the roast pork, yams and taro, they drank some green coconuts and sat around the shade of the sails and started talking.

"At this speed we should be at Sacred Island by this evening. The Seer will probably guide us to him. Most of the island is forest but there are some villages around the fringes. It is mountainous in the interior.", Latou said.

"What do you want us to do father?", 'Etu asked.

"I think we should just follow the Seers guide. He will probably land us on a beach with a track leading to his house. I have heard it is a large compound with many people coming to seek his guidance and advice. There is a kava circle there that is reputed to continue all year round".

They were silent for a moment. The breeze playing with their hair. They were looking towards the horizon now to catch a glimpse of the island. The huge fish has been travelling at the same speed since the morning and it is getting late in the afternoon.

"There it is!", shouted Tupu'a. "I can see the island on the horizon over there!". Tupu'a pointed to a small speck on the horizon.

"Right, it is Sacred Island. The mountain looks like a head looking up at the sky", Latou said.

They were getting excited now. Mafanga prepared their best tapa and wrap around fine mats with coconut sinnet to tie around their waists as a show of respect. They will wear them to the Seer's compound. She also prepared some sweet smelling oils made from candlenut and wild flowers. They will take the oil as presents.

As the island got bigger, their preparations was getting more frenzied.

"Ma, you and Tupu'a serve as guards at the rear. I will lead with 'Etu at the front with Mafanga and Langi in the middle. Sometimes there may be pirates or wild people in the forest who attack visitors to Sacred Island", Latou instructed.

"Alright father", Tupu'a said. He got out his bow and arrows. 'Etu and Ma got their clubs. Latou carries 2 throwing clubs which he can throw at attackers at short distances.

They were ready.

The island was getting closer now. They can see the trees and beaches round it. The Giant Fish headed towards the beach. When they were about 100 arm lengths from shore it dived and let the canoe float.

"Alright, let's paddle the rest of the way", Latou said. "I can see a track going up into the hills. Let's head for it".

The sun was setting and it was getting a bit dark.

# CHAPTER 2.  THE SEER

Once they landed on the beach, Latou organised camp. They collected driftwood on the beach and dry coconut fronds from the surrounding area to build their shelter. They made a large shelter to fit in everyone with two rooms.

They started a fire and cooked some food then settled down for the night. 'Etu, Ma, Tupu'a and Latou will take turns guarding the camp during the night.

Next morning they had a quick breakfast of coconuts and fish they caught in a fish trap. Then they headed into the forest with Latou leading. Tupu'a got out an arrow and was ready to shoot anything that looks threatening. He had learned to shoot with a bow and arrow during his time in Pulotu, the land of the dead. When he returned, Tuputupu Le Fanua the guardian of the entrance to the Spirit World  gave him a bow and arrows. There were only 10 arrows in his quiver, but everytime he takes one out the Gods replace it with a new one. His arrows never miss their mark.

They walked up the mountain. The forest was getting thicker and darker. It would be impossible for anyone to come through it. It was also getting cooler as they went higher.

After half a day, they came to a clearing. There was a Kava circle on it with a large number of participants. There were warriors standing around guarding it with spears and clubs.

"This must be the Seers compound", Latou said as he tries to recover his breath. They can see a large house partly obscured by the trees behind the Kava circle.

"Ma why don't  you go and ask that warrior over there, how we can meet the Seer. There seems to be people everywhere", Latou instructed .

Ma walked up to the warrior and asked. "We are here to seek the wisdom of the Seer. My parents, brothers and sister want to travel to the land of the Gods, but we don't know how. The Seer can tell us how to get there", Ma explained.

"What you seek is not possible. Only the Giant Fish and the Great Wind can take you there. I will guide them". The warrior looked at Ma and he could see stormy seas, sea monsters, whirlpools and a giant bird in his eyes.

Then Ma found himself on the back of the Giant Fish travelling at great speed, holding on to its dorsal fins.

"My brother will take you to the land of the Gods", he could hear the voice saying. He looked around, the canoe was on the back of the fish! Everyone were on board and shouting to him to climb back on board!

Then they heard a roaring sound as if a thousand whales exhaled at the same time. They looked up and saw the clouds gathering in a circle, the sky darkened and the sound grew louder and louder until it was deafening.

"That is Afaa, the Great Wind, my youngest brother", the voice said to Ma. "He will destroy all the monsters in your way so Lupo, the Giant fish, can take you to your destination safely. I will guide you there".

Ma stood up and climbed back into the canoe holding on to the large fish fins on Lupo's back. This kind of magic is new to him and his siblings. They are learning fast.

"The Giant Fish is travelling at great speed. It might be better if we go down below and stay there. It is too windy up here", Mafanga said.

They all went down below deck.

Tupu'a said he will stay on deck as guard with his bow and arrow.

# CHAPTER 3.  THE SEA SERPENT

After 2 days of travelling at high speed on the Giant Lupo's back, Tupu'a noticed a huge head with shining eyes coming towards them as it grew dark, at dusk. It's mouth was opening and shutting. It was large enough to swallow the canoe!

Tupu'a called the rest of the family on deck to watch the huge head as it moved towards them, getting closer and bigger.

"Why don't you shoot its eyes out?", shouted 'Etu over the noise of the wind. Tupu'a shot the monster in the left eye. It roared loudly and lifted its head above the clouds, then came smashing down on the sea in front of them. The wave it created washed over the canoe like a tidal wave. They held on to the mast as the Giant Lupo swerved to avoid the sea serpent. It writhed on the sea surface. Its huge tail swung around missing them as it swept the mast and sail of the canoe into the sea.

"Shoot the other eye as well!", shouted 'Etu again.

Tupu'a got up from the deck where he was sheltering and pulled out another arrow. He waited for the monster to show its head, but it did not. He can only see its back it was turning around looking for them with its good eye under the water. He can see the light from the serpent's eye under the water. He aimed and let fly. The arrow shot through the water, leaving a white trail behind it. They saw the light went out as the monster blinked, then roared even louder as its head shot skywards towards the clouds again.

The arrow found its mark as usual.

The splash was even bigger than before. The Giant Lupo swerving again to avoid being smashed by the monster's body as it landed.  It was probably 50 times bigger than the Giant Lupo.

"You are now safe", the Seer said to Ma. "But I can see a large whirlpool ahead. I will instruct the Giant Lupo to go around it".

The Giant Lupo turned in a wide curve and went east. The Giant Serpent has disappeared.

Probably to lick its wound or its senses has deceived it. It cannot see them anymore. It cannot eat them if it cannot see them.

The wind was getting stronger and louder. The darkening sky now has splashes of lighting flashing behind the clouds without any sound. They all decided to go down below deck and have some sleep. 'Etu will keep watch and take turns with the boys. It must be close to dawn. It is hard to tell as it is always dark and windy.

As the light appears over the horizon 'Etu noticed a huge head rising from the sea. It's the Sea Serpent! It has been following them! He called everyone on board.

"Tupu'a come up quick, it's back! The Sea Serpent. You have to shoot its heart this time", 'Etu shouted.

"Tupu'a and Ma were on the deck in a flash. Tupu'a pulled out another arrow as the monster came closer and opened it's mouth with a roar. The wind became stronger and a gust lifted the monster out of the water but it fell back on the water. The Lupo swerved to avoid the mighty splash.

"Sorry, my brother cannot carry the Sea Serpent. It's too heavy", the Seer said to Ma. "Instruct Tupu'a to shoot one arrow through it's throat to its brain, one arrow through its chest to its first heart and another through its tail where it has a smaller heart", the Seer instructed.

Ma instructed Tupu'a.

"Tupu'a shot one arrow through the serpents's throat. It roared but no sound came out as it splashed back on the sea. The Gian Lupo took another swift turn to avoid being swamped.

22

Tupu'a shot another arrow through the chest and one through the tail. The monster kept coming up but lower each time. Finally it cannot even show its head above water and disappeared in a trail of blood.

# CHAPTER 4. THE SKY MONSTER

After the excitement, they decided to go back down to below deck for another rest. This time Ma will keep watch. It was already light but the wind was still noisy and the dark sky threw shadows over the sea, from clouds gathering on the horizon.

Latou decided to stay on deck as guard. He will call Ma to replace him when he is tired. Ma is the guide, but he also need plenty of rest. The Seer speaks through him.

"I don't think we'll have any more problems to-day", Latou said to Ma. "You might as well sleep for the rest of the day, you need it. We'll try and repair the sail tomorrow, just in case we need it".

"Alright, father", Ma said as they all disappeared into the sleeping quarters.

Latou must have dosed off. He woke when he

fell off his chair. He looked up and saw a huge bird diving towards them. The Giant Lupo must have swerved to avoid his first dive and threw him off his chair.

"Tupu'a, come up here. There is a huge bird diving towards our boat", Latou shouted. "Come up and shoot it down".

The giant bird fixed its eyes on Latou as it followed the Giant Lupo, which was zig zagging across the sea surface.

Tupu'a must have been fast asleep. He cannot hear Latou shouting and calling him. Then the huge bird uttered a frightening, piercing sound almost like a seagull's cry but as loud as a whale blowing by the boat.

Tupu'a stumbled onto the deck. He looked up and saw the bird. "It must be a sea eagle father", he mumbled as he tried to pull out an arrow.

"No, they don't grow that big", Latou shouted back. "It's a monster". Latou was trying to get up and steady himself as he keeps falling over as the Giant Lupo keeps turning.

The huge bird passed over them and turned as the Giant Lupo swerved again to avoid him. Tupu'a shot it on the side, under the wing. It uttered another frightening, piercing cry and disappeared into the clouds.

The commotion had woken everyone. They were all standing around on deck, with cloaks pulled around them. It was beginning to get chilly.

"What happened?", Mafanga asked.

"A giant bird, tried to eat me", Latou said. "Luckily, the Giant Lupo swerved and the bird missed. I was asleep on the chair. It could have carried me off with it. It was probably 4 times bigger than the canoe. Tupu'a shot it and it cried and disappeared into the clouds".

"The bird is coming back. You should all stay below deck. Tupu'a can shoot it through the door as it passes over", the Seer said to Ma. Ma told

everybody and they went below deck.
"Where's Afaa?", asked Langi. "He seemed to
have disappeared. I cannot hear him anymore".

# CHAPTER 5. MAUI, CHIEF OF THE GODS.

"My other brother is leading the way. He is clearing all the dangers for you", the Seer said to Ma. "You will find out why later".

Ma told them.

"Well, that's good. I wonder how many monsters would be in the way if he wasn't clearing the way", Latou said, looking pleased and smiling.

"That bird and the serpent must have been strays".

"What do you think Ma?. Are we almost there? It's been several days, maybe a week now", Tupu'a said.

"You have a few more days to go", the Seer said to Ma. "The Gods know you are coming. They have prepared a feast for you".

"Wow, that will be great. A change of our seafood diet is welcome", Mafanga laughed. They are looking forward to it now, confident in the ability of the three brothers to get them there safely.

The boys already know the limits of their power. It's only when they will something to happen that it happens, like when they turned into a giant to fight the invaders. It seems they have more power together, than apart. But they are happy to let the three brothers help them, they are not ready to tell their parents yet.

It was noticeably getting colder. Latou heated some stones on a fire on the 'umu platform on deck and placed them on a stone platform for that purpose in their sleeping quarters to warm it. Most large Kalias have an 'umu platform, on deck, made of stone for cooking and fires to warm them during the cold nights.

Heating the stones and placing them in the sleeping quarters is an old Polynesian method. The stones will heat up the sleeping quarters and will stay warm for most of the night. The walls are padded with tapa, at night, which keeps the heat inside the room.

They noticed that the sea has also changed colour. It is becoming lighter and there are frequent seagulls flying over them. Seaweeds and other debris also float by as the Giant Lupo continues to carry them without even tiring. The weather during the day is more pleasant with sunshine instead of the dark sky.

"We must be close to the land of the Gods", Latou observed.

"Yes, you will be arriving tomorrow morning. The Giant Fish will let you float by the shore. You can paddle onto the beach where Maui, the Chief of the Gods, is waiting with a welcoming party", the Seer told them through Ma.

They were all excited. Mafanga and Langi started preparing their best tapa and fine mats to wear for the arrival greetings. She wants everyone to look their best in front of the Gods.

She brought out a sweet smelling oil made from rare flowers in the forest for them to use. It was said that a girl using that oil will attract every male to her. The sweet fragrance of the oil will capture their hearts and imagination.

That night, Latou prepared some stones to warm the room. Then they had an evening meal of roasted fish and taro, with the last of their drinking coconuts, in front of the fire on deck. He had built a shelter to keep the wind out. The Giant Lupo is still travelling at the same speed since they started almost 2 weeks ago.

"What shall we say to the Gods?", Mafanga asked Latou.

"Don't worry, they will speak first. Just answer the questions and talk about anything you like", the Seer said through Ma.

"Oh, that's alright then. I want to ask Maui something", Mafanga said, smiling at Langi.

The boys were noticeably quiet that night. It was

almost, as if they know what is going to happen in the land of the Gods.

The next morning, Latou woke up and went up on deck, they were only about 100 arm lengths from shore. The Giant Fish is gone and the boat is just floating on the gentle swells of the sea.

"Boys wake up, we have to start paddling to shore", Latou called from deck.

'Etu, Ma and Tupu'a all came up on deck as fast as they could. They all stood and looked at the green, lush land of the Gods. There is a wide sandy beach right in front of them.

"Start rowing boys, attach the large oars to the side and take turns", Latou said excitedly, fully aware that his boys can row for days without tiring, just like the Giant Fish!

As their canoe got closer to land, they can see a shelter on the beach, just in front of the trees. There seem to be people hurrying around as if in preparation for a great event.

"Come on everyone, you can come down and put on your best tapa and fine mats when you are free. We want to look our best when we arrive", Mafanga said as she disappears below deck.

As they got closer to shore several large, muscular men waded onto the water and grabbed their anchor ropes. They pulled their canoe as close to the beach as they can. Then they attached a platform to the side for them to disembark on. There was a crowd on the beach with three rather tall and muscular men in the finest mats standing at the front.

They all walked down the planks in single file and stood in a line facing the three men and the crowd.

"Welcome to Hawaiki, the land of the Gods", said the man in the middle. "I am Maui. This is Tangaroa"; Maui said, indicating the man on his left… "and this is Hikule'o",… pointing to the man on his right.
"Tangaroa is the God of the sky and Hikule'o is the God of the underworld. I gather you have

met him before", Maui said with a smile.

Latou nodded, not knowing what to say.

"We are pleased that you have made the perilous journey to our shores. Centuries often pass without any visitors. So we have made some exceptions, for you. We will show you around the land of the Gods, but first; do you have anything to say or ask?".

"Yes, your lordship", Mafanga stammered a bit then gained confidence. "I want to ask you to give us a husband for Langi, our daughter. She is a good girl and she helps me a lot, but I think it is time for her to have a husband. Only you, in your infinite wisdom, know what is in a man's heart".

Maui smiled. "I know of 'Etumatupu'a's present. He is right here, on my left".

Latou and Mafanga were so shocked, they could not believe it. 'Etumatupu'a is one of the Gods!

Tangaroa spoke for the first time, smiling at them. "I want to show you around the land of Hawaiki first. Then, I will tell you something more about yourselves, that you do not know yet. Perhaps after that, we can discuss your request again".

Latou and Mafanga both fell on their knees. Tears flowing from their faces. Their knees felt so weak, they could not stand any more. They realise now their children are also Gods! No wonder they can do things that normal people can't. They bowed their heads resting their hands on the sand. Both unable to speak.

Maui spoke again. "The bearers will bring you to the meeting house where we have a feast awaiting you".

The crowd who were standing at the back started chanting as Latou and Mafanga felt themselves being carried on to the carrier box, which is like a giant stretcher with a small house on it. They sat on it, the chanting seem to make them dreamy, they can see that there are people

35

walking beside the carrier. They seem to move like shadows.

They can also see a large house ahead with a large number of people moving around hurriedly as if preparing something, perhaps the food.

'Etu, Ma, Tupu'a and Langi are nowhere to be seen. It is like a coming home feast for them. Now they realise why they want to come here, this is their land; where they came from.

They decided not to mention it to them. They can decide when to tell them their secret.

At the entrance to the meeting house, the carriers put them down and they were directed to the front where a long table heaped with food has been prepared. All sorts of delicacies and all the foods that they can think of were there.

Maui, Tangaroa, Hikule'o, 'Etu, Ma, Tupu'a and Langi were sitting at the middle of the table.

Latou was led to the left side of the table and

Mafanga to the right side. Once seated, they started the feast with some entertainment. The building was filled with people all around. Maybe, hundreds; Latou thought. There was a clearing in the middle in front of the front table for the performers and entertainers. They noticed that most of them seem to float and not actually walking on the ground!

There were dances in groups and singles. There were speeches and comedies. But Latou and Mafanga seem to be in a daze….like in a dream.

Then they saw…what seem to be like a vision…Afaa is flying over the ocean, the sound still deafening like in a storm…and all sorts of monsters falling from the dark clouds that circle in the sky! Hundreds of monsters of all description! There were serpents, large sharks, monster birds and other monsters they don't even know existed! Now they know why no one comes to the land of the Gods…they won't even go past those monsters!

After the feast and the entertainment, they were

shown to their quarters for the night. They were still in a daze....they could not believe some of those things they see.

The room they were in was decorated with fine mats and tapa. Their bed also. It was very warm and cozy, and they fell asleep immediately.

The next morning, they were woken by the sound of women singing from outside the house. It was the sweetest, melodious sound they have ever heard. They quickly put on their best tapa and mats, washing their faces as they move around on a bowl of water for that purpose. They put on some fragrant oils and came outside. There was another feast prepared under a large tree by the house....Miata and the mermaids were sitting under the tree and singing that same song Latou and the kids heard on that stormy night! No wonder he thought it sounded familiar!

"Good morning Latou and Mafanga", Miata greeted them.

"Good morning, Miata. What brings you here?",
Latou stammered, finally finding the confidence
to speak.

"We'll, we are from here!", she laughed, a high
tinkling laugh. "We just came to save you that
night", she said smiling.

"This is my wife Mafanga. You did help us bring
her back from the land of the dead", Latou said
as he looked at her then nodded.

Mafanga sat down and wiped the tears from her
eyes. "I want to thank you for helping my
husband and my children. If it wasn't for your
help, they would not have made it", she said;
crying silently, not even having the courage to
look up.

"We are happy for you Mafanga. Have some
breakfast and the bearers will take you to see the
Gods, who will show you the land of Hawaiki".

Miata waved and they seem to just melt into the
air with her sisters.

Latou and Mafanga helped themselves to the fruits and breakfast provided. There was raw fish, roast pigs, taro leaves in coconut cream, yams, taro, green coconuts and fruits. Mangoes, ripe bananas and plantain and some they haven't seen before.

After breakfast, they washed their hands and mouth as was the tradition. Then they started talking, for the first time since they arrived.

"Now, I am beginning to understand a lot of things about our children", Latou said looking at Mafanga. He told her of what happened when he was blown out to sea. He cannot remember whether he had told her about his encounter with 'Etumatupu'a on Lele-i-Matangi before, but things are much clearer to him now. It was the Gods who answered his prayers and his months of sacrifices. Throwing the fattest and best of his fish into the ocean for them to grant their wish to have children. He is sure the children know a lot more about what is going on than what they are telling them.

They decided not to ask the kids. They will let the kids tell them about it in their own time. Now, they have a secret as well.

The bearers arrived and they got onto it. They carried them to another large house on the compound. The house was empty but there is an entrance into a cave at one end opposite the only door. They were told to sit in the middle of the large house and wait.

They must have dosed off. They suddenly woke with a start, the whole house was moving through the air! Maui, Tangaroa and Hikule'o stood on one side and motioned them to come. The whole side of the house disappeared and they can see everything as if they are on a higher platform moving over the trees!

First they came to a large clearing with thousands of people on it. They appear to be busy making things…like carving…making dolls….images of strange animals and so on… "this is where we create all the living things"….. "humans, animals, plants and other creatures.

The workers here do not get tired, they do not sleep… all they do is create the heavens and the earth and all the living things that you see in it", Maui said pointing at the people below.

Then they moved on to another clearing, there were also thousands of people there…the whole clearing seem to be covered partly in clouds. They appear to be gazing into the clouds and waving their hands as if to clear them…. "These Gods are watching over people in the land of the living. That is why they send the mermaids to save you, because they can see that you were in trouble in the storm", Maui continued.

Then they moved on to the last clearing…there were more people here than the other two clearings….maybe tens of thousands…they seem to be involved in all kinds of activities…."these are the spirits of the living. We look after them here. They can actually control what you do. That is why we know when you ask us something, your spirit comes to see us and make the request. Then we decide to grant or refuse it", Maui said smiling at Latou and Mafanga.

"In your case, we kept refusing to grant your request; then finally Tangaroa decided to come and see you. He created a storm to blow you towards his path so you can talk about your request to have kids. He was moved by your story and decided to grant it. Niutahi is one of us". Maui looked towards the distance and said. "I will send you back to Muifonua. You have seen enough in the land of Hawaiki. Your kids will join you later".

Latou and Mafanga woke up. They have been sleeping under the hibiscus tree by the beach.

"I wonder where the kids have gone", Latou said.

" 'Etu said they will be back in 3 weeks", Mafanga said as she looked out to sea, half hoping to see a sail in the distance.

## CHAPTER 6. THE MASTER PLAN

The Seer was sitting silently on the beach of Sacred Island. He was looking out to sea. Dark clouds were gathering on the horizon and he could hear the distant sound of thunder. Then he saw the large fin sticking out of the water as the Giant Lupo made his way towards him.

The fish came up to the beach and changed into a man, then walked over to where the Seer was sitting.

"Greetings Lupo. Thank you for taking Latou and Mafanga and their children to the land of the Gods", the Seer greeted his brother, who was ripping vines off the forest to cover himself.

"Yes, it was my duty to do your requests. I have one to ask you myself", the Lupo said.

"And what is that?".

"I want you to persuade the girl to marry me. I

am very fond of her. Her parents think, it is time for her to have a husband, but they know she is a God; like you and me. Except that we are half human", Lupo continued. "It would be nice to have a God for a wife. Don't you think?', Lupo smiled at the Seer.

"I can see her. She is in the land of the Gods, talking to Maui. He is the Chief of the Gods. She wants to return to Muifonua to her earth parents, but Maui wants her to stay and carry out the work of the Gods".

"So how can you win a God's hand? How can I ask her to marry me? You know I have been travelling the oceans for thousands of years. You and Afaa have been around for just as long. I finally meet someone I really like", Lupo said looking a bit desperate.

"I am fond of you as well, Lupo. I am really impressed by your bravery and effort in taking us to the land of the Gods", Langi said through the Seer.

"Your highness, you have captured my heart during the two weeks you were riding on my back. After a thousand years in the sea, I want to live on dry land now and enjoy the happiness of a mortal man. Can you grant me that wish?".

"I will have to think about it, Lupo. Discarding eternity to become a mortal is not to be taken lightly", Langi continued. "Even when I am so fond of you and would love to live a mortal's life as your wife, I still have my obligations to the Gods to fulfill".

"Do I take it you will give me an answer soon?", Lupo said; hope showing in his voice.

"Yes, I will give you an answer soon", Langi said brightly.

"We'll Seer, I think that went very well. Can you tell me her answer as soon as you get it?", Lupo asked his brother.

"Yes, I will. I will call you again when that happens". The Seer got up and walked into the forest.

Lupo looked after him as he walked,
remembering their childhood days. Now they
live separate lives. Him in the sea and his brother
up in the mountains of Sacred Island. He also
thinks of his other brother Afaa, he too leads his
own life.

Then he slowly got up and walked into the sea.
Disappearing under the waves.

The Seer was watching him from the forest. He
saw the great fins disappear into the distance,
then he turned and slowly floated up the hill.

THE END…

**Notes on the author...**

 Semisi Pone graduated from the University of Auckland in 1985 with a BSc and in 1989 with a MSc (Hons). He has worked as a Scientist in the Pacific for about 10 years and has travelled extensively during that time. He did some work for MAFF, Tonga. University of the South Pacific. South Pacific Commission and the Food and Agriculture Organisation of the United Nations.

He worked in New Zealand during the past 17 years and he has recorded some of his past experience here. He hopes it will motivate or help other people especially those who struggle to find work.

He has written more than 50 books and ebooks.

They can be found by searching his name in the websites of amazon.com, blurb.com, apple i-bookstores and wheelersbooks.co.nz. There are others who also sell his books in New Zealand.

He has retired from Science and is a full-time writer. He also does some charity work as the Secretary/Treasurer for the Project Revival Charity Trust (Inc). A charity that produces free online books for disadvantaged kids and youth in Northcote, Auckland, New Zealand.

These free online books are also available to everyone on the planet with access to the internet. Simply log into blurb.com and search my name on the website then click on preview on the books you like to read on the list displayed. You can read them for free or buy them.

I hope to produce up to 50 books for this programme known as the "Dreamtime Stories".

Ebooks are not available for reading. Only 10% of the book is displayed.

## OTHER BOOKS FROM RAINBOW ENTERPRISES.

1. Rhymes of an Aspiring Writer+
2. We are all Millionaires+
3. The Children of the Gods. The Beginning.
4. The Children of the Gods. The Invasion.
5. The Children of the Gods. The Hurricane's Brothers
6. The art of feeling great*
7. The Rugby Game (Comedy. EBook)*
8. The $999 million heist (Comedy.EBook)*
9. Poetry in Motion. A selection*
10. Where Broken Dreams Fly. A Novel+
11. Po Malu. A Novel*
12. God is Energy. Do you Believe?+
13. God, Genes, Evolution*
14. The Romance*
15. The Children of the Gods. The Beginning and Invasion+
16. Green Earth. A Poetic Tree+

* - these books can be viewed at Blurb.com. Search the author or title in the public bookstore.
+ - available from amazon.com

## BOOKS ON HUMOR….

1. Jokes from around the Pacific+
2. Jokes from around the Pacific 2
3. Jokes from around New Zealand
4. Jokes from around Australia
5. The book of rugby jokes+
6. The problem drinkers jokebook
7. The quit smoking jokebook
8. The war on drugs jokebook+
9. Jokes from around the USA
10. Jokes from the Land of the Tikongs
11. Jokes from around New Zealand 2
12. The Stupid Idiot's Jokebook
13. Jokes from around the Pacific. A collection

+ - available from amazon.com

www.ingramcontent.com/pod-product-compliance
Lightning Source LLC
Chambersburg PA
CBHW071351130626
46556CB00005B/2136